SHIKARI SH
The Wild Card

WHO ME?

Shikari Shambu is everything he doesn't appear to be.
Just like his name. Although known as Shikari, he is no hunter.
He is a conservationist and a wildlife expert. People turn to him in times of crises.
Whether it is for rescuing a wild animal or catching a dangerous criminal, this forest
ranger is everybody's go-to guy. But, lo and behold, Shambu is no brave heart. He is
secretly petrified of animals and has no love for adventure. All he seeks is a good,
fluffy pillow to sleep on. But trouble always finds its way to Shambu and luck finds
him a way out. And the combination of the two creates a hilarious mad-venture!

Created by former *Tinkle* editor, Luis Fernandes, and brought to life by
V.B. Halbe, Shikari Shambu is one of the most popular characters in the *Tinkle* stable.
Over 30+ years, he has had many adventures and run-ins with the wildest and most
exotic of animals, birds, insects, plants, and, occasionally, humans. Illustrated by
Savio Mascarenhas since 1998, Shambu has only gone from funny to funnier.

Readers Speak:

"Shikari Shambu makes me want to go on a jungle adventure." **– Deepali Gupta,** *via email*

"My classmates thanked me for introducing them to Shikari Shambu. They all simply loved his tales." **– C. Neha,** *Tamil Nadu*

"Shambu's stories are always thrilling and it makes me think that Shambu should become an actor." **– Namita K.,** *Bengaluru*

"The stories of Shikari Shambu are always humorous." **– Aniket Sanyal,** *Kolkata*

"Savio Sir, in every Shikari Shambu comic, there is always a small bird or bunny or squirrel passing by and watching his
adventures. These are not part of the story but without them it doesn't look like a Shambu comic. Thank you for drawing
them." **– Aaditya Nair,** *via email*

"I love Shikari Shambu episodes. I wait for the clever way he tackles those who harm animals." **– Joshua Sundaram,** *via email*

SOMEWHERE IN THE JUNGLES OF MASABA...

Shambu
The Wrestler

Writer: Sharmistha Sinha
Illustrator: Savio Mascarenhas
Colourist: Umesh Sarode

CUT. EXCELLENT SHOT, MR. SHAMBU. LET'S BREAK FOR LUNCH.

(COUGH COUGH)

TED, YOU'VE BEEN COUGHING FOR MONTHS. DO SOMETHING ABOUT IT.

HEY ACHMED, DID YOU GET MY MEDICINE?

YEAH, TED. HERE IT IS — TRADITIONAL JUNGLE MEDICINE MADE OF WILD HONEY AND HERBS.

ACTION!

????

GRRROWLLL

HMPH, I CAN DO THAT BETTER...

GGGRROOWWLLL

GRRRRRR...

WOW. THEY'RE REALLY INSPIRED. KEEP THE CAMERAS ROLLING.

WHAT FOLLOWED WAS SOMETHING NO ONE EVER FORGOT...

YOU DON'T FRIGHTEN ME!

thump!

7

CUT! BRAVO... BRAVO!! BRILLIANT PERFORMANCE, TED!!!

CLAP
CLAP.
CLAP.

HEY TED, YOU CAN GET UP NOW. TED!

SOMEONE CALLED ME? SORRY, I FELL ASLEEP IN THE TRAILER.

IF THAT'S TED, THEN WHO IS...

AAAAGHHHH

ZZZZZZ

THE NEWS SPREAD LIKE WILDFIRE...

TODAY, THE GREAT SHIKARI SHAMBU KNOCKED OUT A BEAR IN A BAREHANDED WRESTLING MATCH. HERE'S AN ACCOUNT...

Click

SOMEWHERE IN THE BACKYARD...

COUGH COUGH.

MY POT OF MEDICINE. IT'S EMPTY!

9

13

Hats Off!

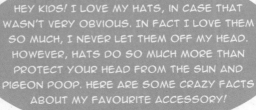

HEY KIDS! I LOVE MY HATS, IN CASE THAT WASN'T VERY OBVIOUS. IN FACT I LOVE THEM SO MUCH, I NEVER LET THEM OFF MY HEAD. HOWEVER, HATS DO SO MUCH MORE THAN PROTECT YOUR HEAD FROM THE SUN AND PIGEON POOP. HERE ARE SOME CRAZY FACTS ABOUT MY FAVOURITE ACCESSORY!

Text: Amanda D'souza
Illustrations & Design: Savio Mascarenhas

Did you know that the traditional white hat that chefs wear has 100 pleats? These 100 pleats represent the 100 various ways in which an egg can be cooked. Yummy! I love it when two of my favourite things combine!

Different coloured hats seen at construction sites serve a specific purpose. White hard hats are worn by supervisors or engineers, blue by technical advisers. Safety inspectors wear green hard hats. Yellow hard hats are worn by labourers while orange or pink is reserved for new workers or visitors. I wish animals had a similar system, so that I'd know which ones are safe and which want me for lunch.

A Frenchman, Louis Comte, was the first man to pull a rabbit out of a hat in 1814 during a magic show! You could say this was the first 'hat' trick!

Hat etiquette states that one must always remove one's hat when the national anthem is being played. Hats off to my nation!

The bowler hat was designed in 1849 by the London hat makers Thomas and William Bowler. This tough, low-rise hat was meant to protect people on horseback from low-hanging branches. I wear my own trusty brown cover for similar reasons. However, sometimes, those wretched branches smack my face anyway!

Story
Jayashree Nair

Script
Rajani Thindiath

Illustrator
Savio Mascarenhas

Colourist & Letterer
Jyotsna Patel

19

20

Shikari Shambu Dino Land

Story & Script
Rajani Thindiath

Art
Savio Mascarenhas

Letters
Prasad Sawant

SHAMBU WAS IN THE US VISITING HIS FRIEND, PROFESSOR STEIN, THE ECCENTRIC MILLIONAIRE SCIENTIST...

COME ALONG, I'LL SHOW YOU MY COLLECTION OF NATURAL HISTORY EXHIBITS.

NATURAL HISTORY, PROF. STEIN! WHEN DID YOU DEVELOP AN INTEREST IN NATURAL HISTORY?!

I'VE ALWAYS BEEN INTERESTED IN THE SUBJECT BUT IT'S ONLY IN THE LAST 10 YEARS THAT I'VE STARTED COLLECTING!

THIS I HAVE TO SEE!

NOT A MACHINE PRECISELY... IT'S MORE OF AN INVISIBLE WARP... I WAS DOING SOME EXPERIMENTS IN HERE AND, FOR THE LIFE OF ME, I CAN'T REMEMBER WHERE I LEFT IT!

WHAT DOES IT DO?

NOW, BE CAREFUL HERE, I HAD MISPLACED A TIME MACHINE SOMEWHERE AROUND...

YOU MISPLACED A TIME MACHINE?!

IF YOU PASS THROUGH IT AND IF IT IS TIMED FOR A PARTICULAR DATE, IT WILL TAKE YOU BACKWARD OR FORWARD IN TIME.

O... KAY!

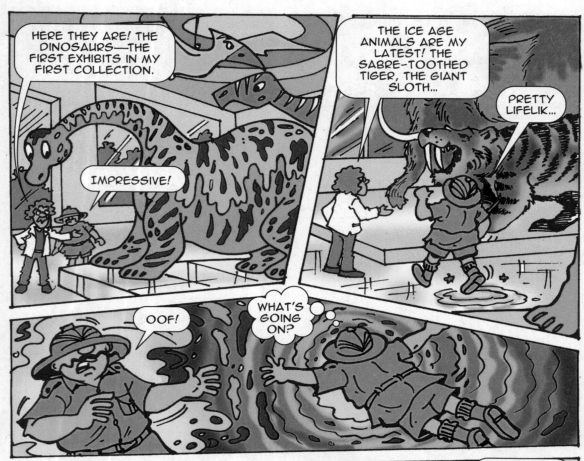

22

*SHORT FOR TYRANNOSAURUS REX,
A CARNIVOROUS DINOSAUR

25

DE-PATHED!

READERS! I NEED YOUR HELP! I AM SUPPOSED TO CAPTURE BHAYANAK KHAUF, THE DREADED SMUGGLER AND POACHER WHO IS ENDANGERING THE ANIMALS IN KADE JUNGLE! I CHASED HIM TO A CLEARING, AFTER WHICH HE TOOK ONE OF THESE FOUR ROADS. HELP ME DECIDE WHICH PATH LEADS TO BHAYANAK! CHOOSE WISELY, FOR HE HAS SET UP TRAPS FOR ME AT THE END OF ALL THE OTHER PATHS! DO NOTE: THESE ROADS ARE QUITE TRICKY, THEY GO OVER, AROUND AND EVEN UNDER EACH OTHER. SO STAY SHARP!

Concept & Text: Amanda D'souza
Illustrations: Anupama Apte
Layout: Jitendra Patil

Shikari Shambu
The Big Burp Theory

Story, Pencils & Inks	Script	Colours	Letters
Savio Mascarenhas	Dolly Pahlajani	Snehangshu Mazumder	Pranay Bendre

Rrruuumble!
Rrrrumble!

OOPS, SORRY... AGAIN! EHEHE!

SOON—

BUGLE! SO GOOD TO SEE YOU. IT'S BEEN SO LONG! HOW'S YOUR MARINE RESEARCH GOING?

I'LL TELL YOU WHEN WE REACH THE DOCKS.

HERE WE ARE.

OH DEAR. THAT LOOKS A LOT LIKE THE SHIP IN MY DREAM...

SO, WHAT EXACTLY HAVE YOU CALLED ME FOR?

SEE THIS? IT'S THE PROBE WE LOWER INTO THE DEPTHS OF THE SEA. IT HAS A CAMERA ATTACHED THAT ALLOWS US TO STUDY MARINE PLANTS.

LAST WEEK, WE WERE FAR OUT IN THE PACIFIC OCEAN WHEN SOMETHING SNAPPED OFF THE HEAD OF THE PROBE. SOMETHING... **POWERFUL**.

29

WE COULD HEAR SOME AWFUL RUMBLING AND THE SHIP BEGAN SWAYING VIOLENTLY.

JUST LIKE IN MY DREAM!

WHEN WE RETURNED TO SHORE, I FOUND OUT THAT THE SPOT IS CALLED THE 'GREAT PACIFIC GARBAGE PATCH'*, ONE OF THE WORLD'S LARGEST PLASTIC DUMPS.

SO I PUT TOGETHER A TEAM OF SCIENTISTS AND WE'RE GOING TO INVESTIGATE THE AREA.

THEN YOU DON'T REALLY NEED ME, DO YOU?

WE CAN'T RULE OUT THE POSSIBILITY OF A MUTATED ANIMAL-TURNED-MONSTER. YOU, MY FRIEND, ARE MY RESIDENT ANIMAL EXPERT.

M—MUTANT? M—M—MONSTER?

DR. BUGLE, WE'VE PULLED UP ANCHOR.

GREAT, CAPTAIN.

NO, IT ISN'T... WE MIGHT NEVER RETURN.

*HTTP://EN.WIKIPEDIA.ORG/WIKI/GREAT_PACIFIC_GARBAGE_PATCH

AFTER A FEW DAYS AT SEA...

LOOK THERE. GARBAGE HAS STARTED SHOWING UP AGAINST THE SHIP. WE MUST BE CLOSE.

OH CRAP!

SERIOUSLY. HOW CAN PEOPLE DUMP CRAP INTO SUCH BEAUTIFUL OCEANS!

SIR, IT'S GETTING DARK. I SUGGEST WE CONTINUE OUR SEARCH TOMORROW.

YES, YES. LET'S.

IT'S ALL RIGHT, CAPTAIN. THE CAMERA IS EQUIPPED FOR LOW LIGHT. BESIDES, OUR SHIP'S GOT FLOODLIGHTS TOO.

PROBE BEING LOWERED INTO THE SEA. STANDBY FOR CAMERA FEED.

HERE'S THE CAMERA FEED. KEEP YOUR EYES OPEN, PEOPLE.

THRASH!

DID YOU SEE THAT? SOMETHING'S DEFINITELY OUT THERE! SOMETHING BIG.

31

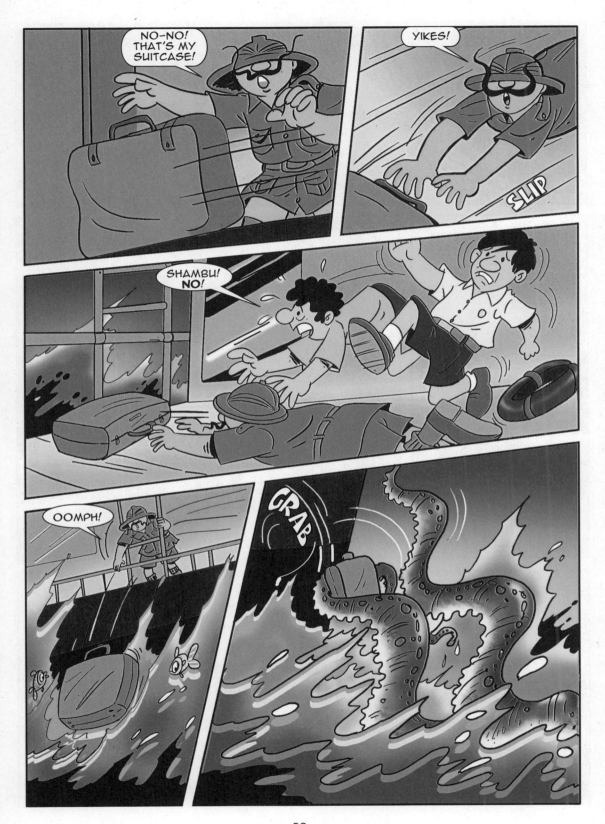

RRRRRUMBLE

YIIEEE! THE CAPTAIN WAS RIGHT! IT'S A **MONSTER**! IT'S PULLING THE WHOLE SHIP INTO THE OCEAN. WHICH MEANS I'M GETTING CLOSER TO IT!

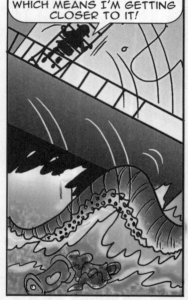

STOP! STOP!

HUH? IT STOPPED? IT *HEARD* ME? MAYBE...

OKAY, NOW L-LET GO OF THE SHIP!

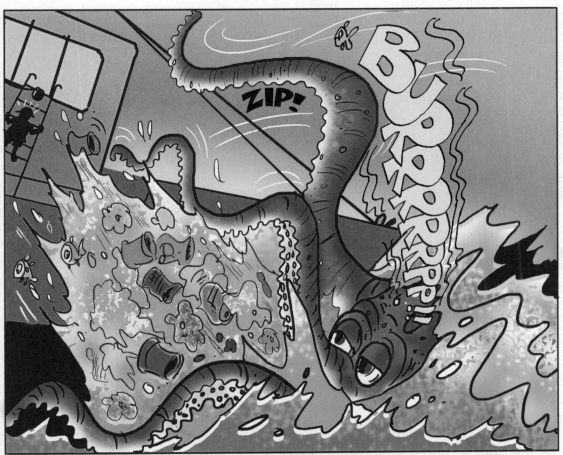

FIRST, LET'S GET SOME HELP TO EXTRACT OUR 'MONSTER'.

THWACK!

OWWW!

GUESS IT DOESN'T LIKE BEING CALLED A MONSTER. HEHEHE.

AND SO, THEY RADIOED FOR HELP. A HUGE FISHNET WAS USED TO FISH OUT THE GIANT SQUID, WHICH WAS SET FREE IN THE CLEANER PART OF THE PACIFIC.

DR. BUGLE, SHAMBU, AND A SMALL TEAM OF SCIENTISTS AND VOLUNTEERS SET ABOUT CLEARING UP THE AREA.

I JUST NEED TO POUR THIS CHEMICAL IN... IT WILL CAUSE THE PLASTICS TO GEL TOGETHER AND WE CAN PULL THEM OUT...

AND IF YOU FIND ANY TRAPPED ANIMAL, GIVE IT SHAMBU'S SPECIAL DOSE...

BURRP!

The Pun Is Mightier Than The Sword.

Puns: Amanda D'souza   Illustrations: Priya Panicker   Layout: Jitendra Patil

WHAT DO YOU CALL A SCARY SHIKARI SHAMBU? SHIKARI SHAM'BOO'.

OH NO! NOT ANOTHER TEDDY-BORE!

WHY DOES SHAMBU HATE TEDDIES? HE CAN'T 'BEAR' THE SIGHT OF THEM.

WHY DOES SHAMBU LOVE SLEEPING IN THE JUNGLE? BECAUSE IT IS FOR-REST.

NOW, THAT IS MOOSE TO ME!

WHAT DO YOU CALL AN ELK'S HAIRY UPPER LIP? MOOSE-TACHE.

BURRRP! OOPS HEHEHE!

WHAT DO YOU CALL AN EMBARRASSED BIRD? (H)AWKWARD.

OOOPS! I'VE BEEN SPOTTED!

WHICH ANIMAL IS KNOWN TO COPY DURING EXAMS? THE CHEETAH.

SHIKARI SHAMBU — Jumbo Adventure in Assam

Story & Script
Anisha H. Karthick

Pencils & Inks
Savio Mascarenhas

Colours
Pranay Bendre & Umesh Sarode

Letters
Prasad Sawant

BINOO, PRINCESS... THESE ARE DADDY'S FRIENDS, SHAMBU UNCLE AND SHANTI AUNTY.

HI!

AWW! SO CUTE.

THE NEXT DAY—

DO YOU HAVE THE FOUR-HEADED HORSE DOLL IN TERRACOTTA?

SHANTI SHOPS AS IF THERE'S NO TOMORROW. SHEESH!

NO, MA'AM. IT'S BEEN OUT OF STOCK FOR MONTHS.

WHAT!

YES... IT'S A COMPLICATED DESIGN THAT ONLY THE BEST OF ARTISTS ATTEMPT.

WHY DON'T YOU TRY AT SOME OTHER SHOP?

MORE SHOPS?!

DEAR, HOW ABOUT BUYING THIS NORMAL HORSE, INSTEAD?

I'M NOT LEAVING THIS MARKET UNTIL I GET MY FOUR-HEADED HORSE!

40

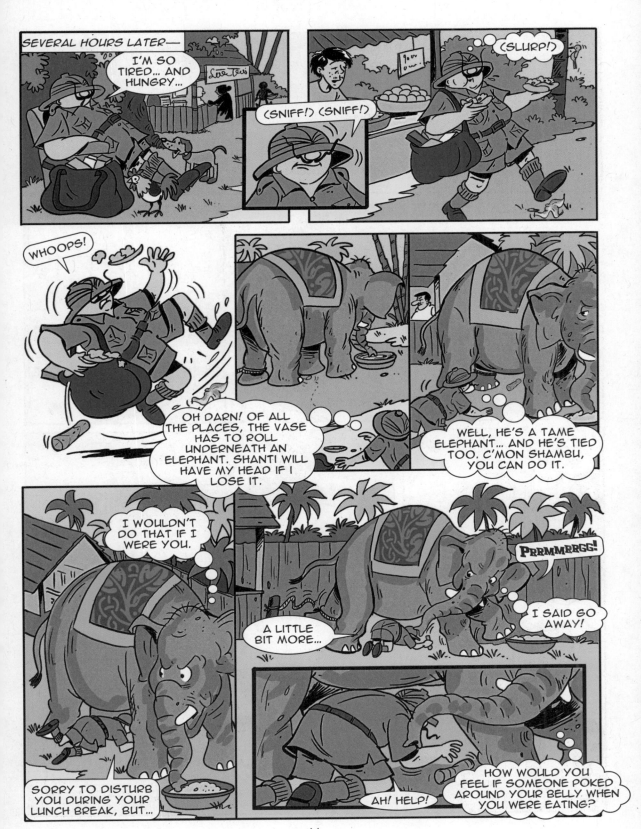

41

43

44

A WEEK LATER—

TIME FLIES SO QUICKLY WHEN YOU ARE WITH FRIENDS.

WE HAD SUCH A NICE TIME HERE, DEBEN.

YEAH... I'M GOING TO MISS THE QUIET NAPS, THE ASSAMESE SNACKS, AND...

WAIT!

THE FOUR HEADED HORSE! HOW? WHERE...?!

MY WIFE MAKES TERRACOTTA DOLLS... I OVERHEARD YOU THE OTHER DAY.

OH! YOU SHOULDN'T HAVE...

IT'S JUST A SMALL GESTURE OF GRATITUDE, FOR CALMING APPU THAT DAY.

YOU CALMED HIM?! BUT, I THOUGHT APPU HAD DROPPED YOU ON MY ORDERS.

BINODINI, MY LOVE!

(SIGH) I TAKE THE TROUBLE TO CALM YOU AND SHANTI GETS THE FANCY GIFT! HUMPH!

SHIKARI SHAMBU   CUB SCOUTS

Story
Savio & Sean

Script
Sean D'mello

Pencils & Inks
Savio Mascarenhas

Colours
Lidwin Mascarenhas

Letters
Pranay Bendre

ONE FINE EVENING...

YUMMY FOOD, LONG UNEVENTFUL NAPS AND NO ANIMALS IN SIGHT. I COULD GET USED TO MUMBAI AND THIS LIFE!

LATER THAT NIGHT—

TING TONG!

I'M COMING, I'M COMING!

COGITO ERGO SUM!

THEY WEREN'T JOKING WHEN THEY SAID THIS CITY NEVER SLEEPS.

MR. SHAMBU, YOU MUST HELP US! A LEOPARD CUB HAS BEEN SPOTTED IN OUR COLONY.

COGITO ERGO SUM!

ALL THE RESIDENTS HAVE LOCKED THEIR HOUSES AND ARE REFUSING TO COME OUT.

WE KNOW IT'S NOT AS EXCITING AS THE ANIMALS YOU USUALLY ENCOUNTER, BUT WILL YOU COME WITH US AND RESCUE THE ANIMAL?

HEHE, SURE.

GREAT! NOW HOW DO I GET OUT OF THIS ONE?

AND SO, WITH THE 'FEARLESS' SHIKARI SHAMBU BY THEIR SIDE, THE RESIDENTS START THEIR SEARCH—

HOW DID A LEOPARD ENCROACH ON OUR RESIDENTIAL COLONY ANYWAY?

SEE THAT NATIONAL PARK AROUND THE COLONY? **WE** ARE THE ENCROACHERS HERE.

POOR LEOPARD DOESN'T KNOW THAT PEOPLE LIVE HERE. HE'S JUST COME OUT FOR A NIGHT STROLL.

Gymnasti

WELL, HERE WE ARE. THIS IS WHERE THE ANIMAL WAS LAST SPOTTED.

48

NATURAL HEROES

Shambu: The wild is filled with some amazing animals. Beautiful creatures that are strong, majestic and, sometimes, adorable. Many people have worked tirelessly over the years to keep both the fierce as well as the cuddly creatures safe in their natural habitat. Most of these green legends have inspired me too! Today, I'd like to introduce you to some of my herbiheroes!

Rachel Carson: An American marine biologist, environmentalist and a writer, Ms. Carson's activism helped the world become aware of the damaging effects of pesticides and fertilizers on our delicate ecosystem. Her book, *Silent Springs*, helped the world become more environmentally conscious, and alerted us to the dangers of pollution. Her writing is considered to be the most influential of its kind, even today. Her writing is so easy to follow and so engaging, that even I enjoyed it!

David Attenborough: Known widely as 'the Godfather of natural history TV', Sir Attenborough was (and still is) responsible for stirring the first real enthusiasm for wildlife amongst TV viewers. He managed to enthrall his audience with his distinctly captivating voice-overs that provided an insight into the lives of the animals he studied. His entertaining and easy presentations made all his natural history shows unforgettable. His passion and love for animals is highly contagious! I am guilty of having caught some of it!

Jane Goodall: At age 26, Jane Goodall did something that I would NEVER dare to do at any age: she decided to live with chimpanzees to observe their behaviour. With patience and hope, this animal rights activist successfully published her findings and gave biologists the world over an insight into the lives of these primates. Goodall urged the African nations to develop nature-friendly tourism programmes. Today, she is considered the foremost authority on primatology* and animal conservation.

Gerald Durell: Born in India, Gerald Durell grew up to be a famous naturalist, conservationist, zookeeper, and wildlife TV presenter. He founded the Jersey Zoo as a centre for the conservation of endangered animals. Durell offered a humorous insight into the world of animals. His funnily discritive writing made him one of the most popular wildlife authors of all time. Besides tirelessly working for animals, he trained people from around the world to save animals in their own countries. His books helped create several environmentalists, myself included. Hehehe.

Jim Corbett: Mr. Corbett is arguably one of the most recognized conservationists in India, and my biggest inspiration. Corbett first entered the spotlight as a hunter but later move on to giving public lectures about the importance of conservation. He was the first to initiate the establishment of a bird sanctuary in 1933 at Nainital within the boundaries of the municipality where killing of wild animals and birds was forbidden. He created the All-India Conference for the Preservation of Wild Life and the Hailey National Park, which was later renamed in his honour. I wonder if Kalia will rename Big Baan in my honour!

*study of primates

Text: Amanda D'souza   Layout: Jitendra Patil

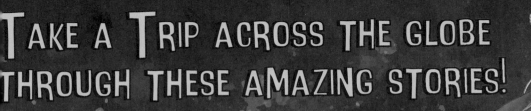

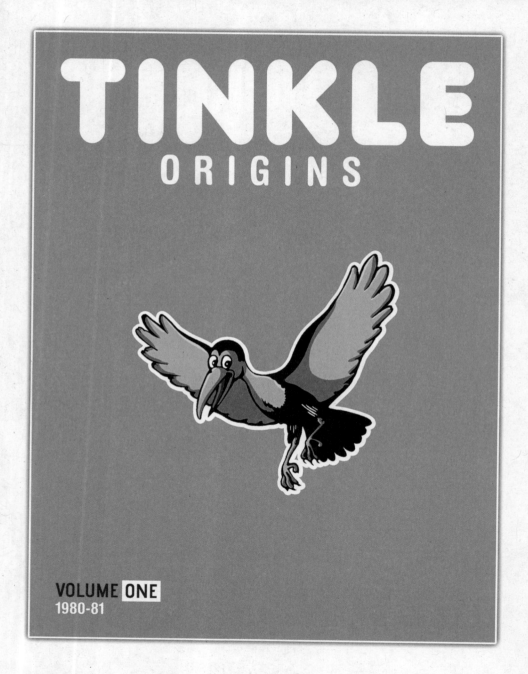

SHIKARI SHAMBU
CHANCE MEETINGS

Story & Script
Dolly Pahlajani

Pencils & Inks
Savio Mascarenhas

Colours
Akshay Khadilkar

Letters
Prasad Sawant

Crack!

(HUFF-PUFF!)

DARN THIS RAIN AND DARN THIS FOREST. I COULDN'T HAVE CHOSEN A WORSE TIME TO LOSE MY WAY.

Crack!

COULDN'T HAVE SPOTTED IT AT A BETTER TIME. I'LL GO AND ASK FOR SHELTER.

WHAT'S THAT? A HOUSE IN THE MIDDLE OF NOWHERE?

Knock! Knock!

ANYONE HOME? PLEASE HELP ME!

55

*SOMEONE WHO PREPARES, STUFFS, AND MOUNTS THE SKINS OF ANIMALS WITH LIFELIKE EFFECT

Shikari Shambu
The Wild Cat

Writer
Ravi Sinha

Pencils & Inks
Savio Mascarenhas

Colours
Umesh Sarode

Letters
Pranay Bendre

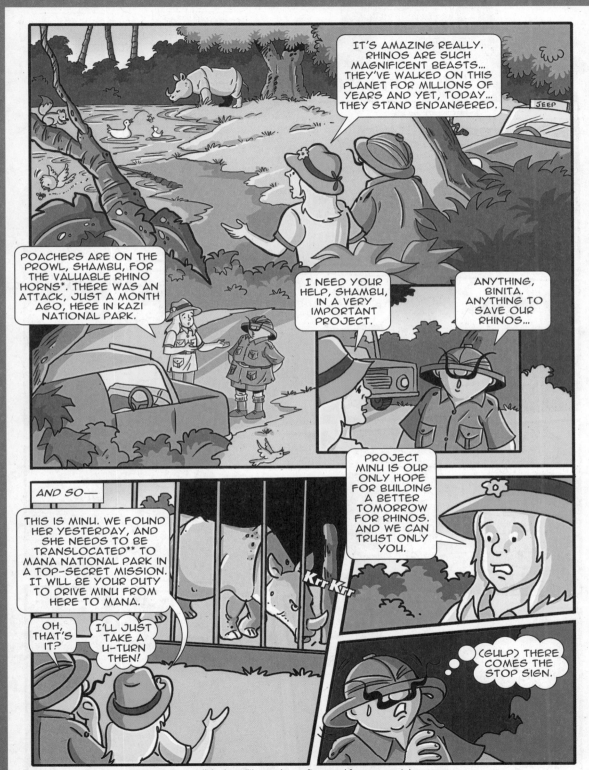

*Rhino horns are supposed to have medicinal qualities and are often used for ornamental purposes
**Animals are often moved to various other habitats to expand the distribution and population of the animal

Shikari Shambu
PROJECT MINU

Story & Script
Shruti Dave

Pencils & Inks
Savio Mascarenhas

Colours
Akshay Khadilkar

Letters
Prasad Sawant

MOVING DAY—

MINU WILL BE SAFE AND COMFORTABLE IN THIS BOX. NOW REMEMBER, SHAMBU, DON'T TRUST ANYONE. ONCE YOU REACH MANA NATIONAL PARK, THE FOREST OFFICIALS THERE WILL HELP YOU WITH MINU.

BUT WHO'LL HELP ME ALL THE WAY TILL MANA?

THERE'S A RHINO IN MY TRUCK! AND IT'S TOO LATE TO PASS THE BUCK! I CAN'T BELIEVE THERE'S A RHINO IN MY TRUCK!

HUH? LOOKS LIKE SOMEONE'S HAVING CAR TROUBLE...

THANKS FOR STOPPING. OUR CAR BROKE DOWN. CAN YOU HELP US?

SURE.

RIGHT. I'LL BE BACK IN A MINUTE. STAY RIGHT HERE.

SAY, WHAT ARE YOU CARRYING IN THAT BIG TRUCK?

ERM, NOTHING. JUST SOME... TEA LEAVES.

OKAY!

MAN, I'M HUNGRY.

67

70

71